11:11

11:11

11:11
By Kayil York

Cover design: Mitch Green
Artwork: Muhammed Salah

11:11

11:11 playlist

Power Over Me by Dermot Kennedy
Read About Memory by Donovan Woods
Untitled by Billie Marten
Cologne by Haux
Q (The Best One Of Our Lives) by Evans Blue
Whiskey (Lost Recording #5) by Mark Diamond
Shelter by Dermot Kennedy
Where You Are by Mayday Parade
You're Special by NF
Whiskey and Morphine by Alexander Jean
Goodnight Moon by Go Radio
Looks Red, Tastes Blue by Mayday Parade
Slip by Elliot Moss
Mercy by Lewis Capaldi
October by George Ogilvia
Reveries by Bones & Bridges
Lost by Dermot Kennedy
Let Go by Frou Frou

11:11

To the lovers that are meant to be.
I pray you never let go of each other.

11:11

11:11

"I fell in love with his soul
before I could even touch his skin.
If that isn't true love,
then please tell me what is."

11:11

When it comes to your love,
show me no mercy.
I want it all.

#youaremyeverything

This idea of the heart is both reckless and madness. For it pulls and pushes and aches and gives so much of itself for love. Even after it's been broken, the will to keep giving is as sure as the sky is pinned to the atmosphere.

To have anything of value,
sacrifices must be made.
Time, effort, connection.
This is how you figure out
what it worth losing in order
to gain something that has
the power to change your life.

I will never be sorry for the way I have chosen to love with no condition. It has made my heart expand so wide; I was sure nothing more could make it grow. Until I made a promise to love him for always. When a bond like that is forged and the wine is washed down with spoken promises, you die to yourself in order to serve something greater than your own self, your own heart, and your own life.

You put aside selfishness to be selfless. It doesn't mean you stop being yourself or stop becoming more of who you are. It is the concept of sharing yourself with someone else so you both can grow and change, while being together. Opening yourself up to something above yourself is the greatest form of ascension you can do in this world.

Because it is the greatest way of becoming, growing, and knowing what real love is.

The way you are meant to love, is the way you are meant to breathe; necessary to live each day through. The comfort of a blanket that sits like faithful security on top of you through the night. It is the way you have faith in the sun to rise in the morning because of the expectation that life continues. This is how you love; the way you breathe, without question.

These days will shift
from good to bad,
bad to good,
heaven to hell,
hell to heaven.
A consistent change
that shows us how
strong we can be
and become,
even while we're
happy, even while
we're sad.

You're in the fabric of my favorite blue shirt
because it holds the places where your hands
have touched and held me when the pieces of
my world were crumbling down.
And for this, I can't unlove you.

#yourimprint

I become something more as these moments pass. Because I am willing myself to be more. And I am ok with being someone you have never known. Mainly, because it will be the chance to be more of myself. I need that.

There wasn't a need for words, but when they spilled from your mouth, I could not help but eat each one like the pieces of the moon when I needed my soul to glow.

Oh, the lengths we go to carry on.
The things we do for the ones we love;
in never letting go and always hanging on.

Sit with me and rearrange the stars in our
room, just like this rearranging of life to bring
us closer together. Lay here with me so we can
share this memory of tangling ourselves up in
simple laughter and sacred secrets.
Kissing so deeply until the sun comes up
to splash our sheets with golden hues.

#moonbeamlover

And I haven't thought about what may happen when the night comes for us. I just know that I'm here to stay forever with you, sweet darling. Just as the stars stay alongside the moon. We are meant to be here, in the same room.

I love too much.
Trust me, I know.
But I can't change
what's burned into
my very bones.

Somehow you made the brokenness inside me feel like a valid limb that should be loved just as much as the heart beating inside my chest. Somehow you made me love myself more than I ever thought could be possible. You are immeasurable to me in this human form.

The heart is a funny thing.
The way it pulls you to do
everything under the sun.
And love beyond our own
capabilities.

If there were arms that could cradle me more than this, I would doubt it. Because nothing feels as authentic as the way your fingers caress the miles of this skin.

She was drawn to the things,
the spaces, the magic of untouched skies
and the kind of stars that held 11:11 wishes.

Darling,
you know
me well.
So I don't
have to tell
you how much
my heart
beats
beats
beats
for your
next breath.
Just look
at me,
please.
And for
tonight,
dance
with my
eyes.

The terrible truth of it,
is that I would choose
the hurt in the end if it
meant loving you
in the in between.
Because a little bit
of pain is nothing
compared to the joy
of sweet, sweet love.

How beautiful is it,
to lie on your back
and make wishes on
stars that give
the secrets of heaven?

Whether you keep me with you or not,
I'd give you my pieces all over again.
Because I don't need to be kept
in order to make the decision
to love you.

She was the kind of universe that's
a brand-new version of what you don't
know you need.

I still felt like crying after we talked about the struggles we've been going through lately. But you still feel like home when you wrapped me in your arms and kissed my shoulder like the promise of ok.

This beauty of sorts is dancing inside your smile.
And oh, how I long to help create something
everlasting with it.

Grow old with me,
with the endless
morning coffee
and dried roses
between book pages.
Grow old with me,
in flannel blankets
and snuggles on
Sunday mornings.
Grow old with me,
under star lit skies
and bottles of wine.
Grow old with me,
doing all the things
we dreamed about
while we were young.

#burgeon

This old heart is bruised
along with the colors
of the night sky.
But that's what makes
it so damn beautiful to see.
That even though something
can be made out of the colors of bruising,
doesn't mean it stops being worthy.

When I tell you I love you, that means I care to such a degree that holds no condition. It means that you can trust me with your pieces and all your uncertainties. Because I would never use them against you.

When I tell you I love you, I am all in and would go through any kind of hell to keep you safe from harm. And I would endure hell with you if I couldn't keep it from finding you. I will never give up on you, no matter how hard these days get. All because the love I have for you is greater than the imperfections that you think don't make you worth it.

If there is peace to be had,
it's in being kept.
Being held by a soul whether
the body is present or not.

Stay in this quiet with me.
Soak into me as I watch
your lips move to the taste
of my silhouette.

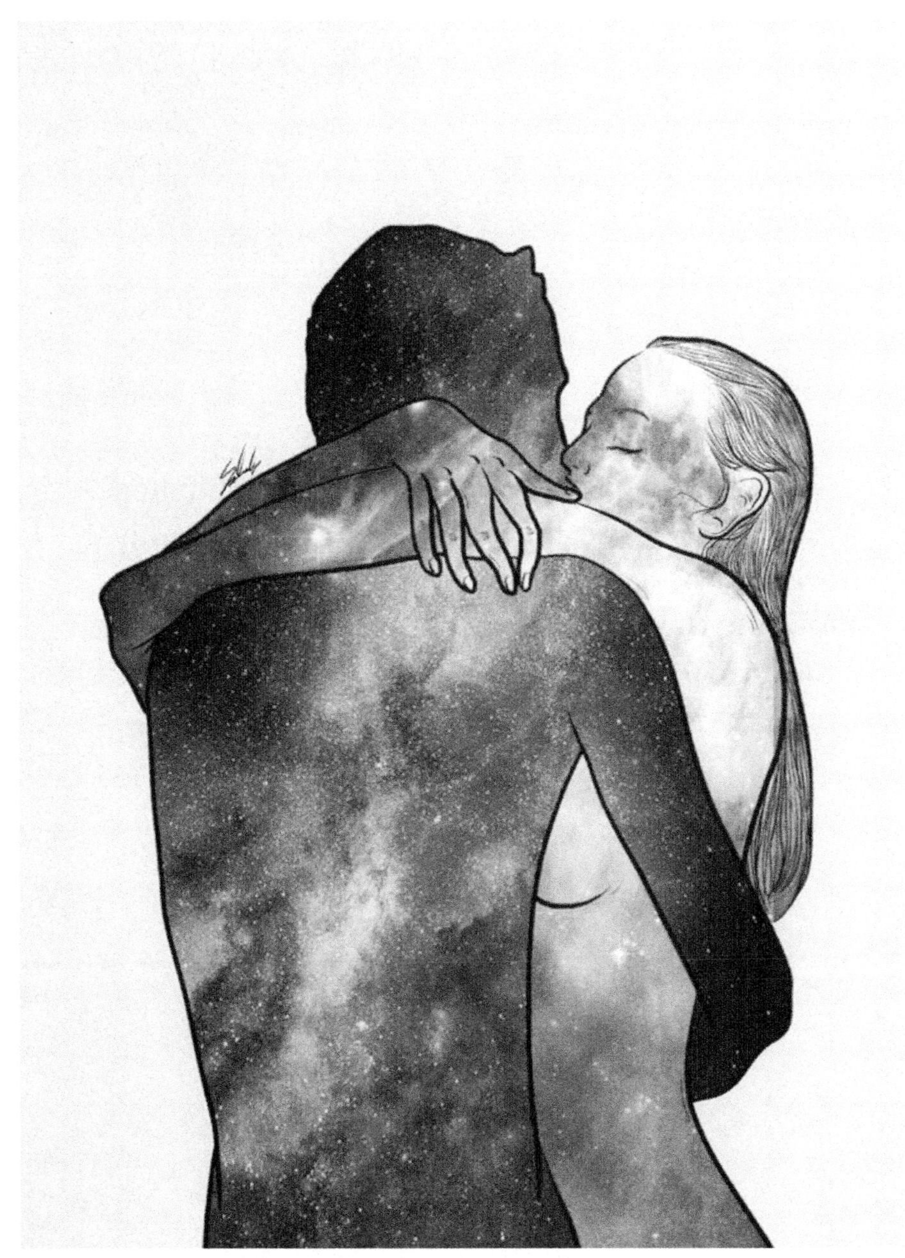

You unlocked galaxies inside of me that birthed a new way to see life in all its glory. Not only because I have you, but because I was becoming more me than I had previously allowed.

Those who are able to love through the things they don't feel they can, are the strongest. Because it takes strength to love people when you are weak. And it takes strength to love through the flaws. But that's when you know how deep the connection truly is.

Give me the kind of love that kills. That twists my soul up like a tornado and slams me into a million pieces.
I want to break, and crack, and crumble in hands that know how to put me back together.
Give me the kind of love that will erupt my very foundation and shake me to the core so I can feel what it's like to be truly awakened.

Dance with me now,
and let's make the stars fall
until our bodies are
drenched in light.

#stelliferous

In a world full of uncommitted people, she just wants something strong. Someone who not only stays but makes it easy to see how much they want themselves to stay present.

She wants someone who isn't afraid of running from the fire, but that stands by her as they face it together. There are too many weak things in this world, and for once it would be nice to have something truly solid.

Forget the promises.

Love me the way the day
comes after the night.
Consistently.

You have been brave your entire life. It's not that you wanted to be, but life gave you no other option. For a while it wasn't the easiest way to maneuver through, but it didn't matter the way your heart tore, you took your tattered edges and put them together and formed a beautiful mosaic. You don't like to flaunt it very much, because the time it took to piece yourself together was in and of itself a battle. And not everyone is worthy of seeing the vulnerable edges we fought so hard to keep from bleeding. It takes a special kind of soul to know who you truly are, the way you think, and the way you process life. But that is what makes you so incredibly special to know, after you fight your way through the walls, your soul will not have to protect itself as if it would be harmed.

It’s simple really.
Keeping you this close.
It’s not that I need you,
it’s the fact that all I do
is choose you.
Because I want to.

You have a home deep within me. I love you like hurricanes need water in order to become something huge and worth giving a name to. We own who we are and give everything we have to be there for one another despite the chaos that constantly surrounds us.
I love you, because you are worth loving in your entirety. And at the end of the day, I would trade anything in order to keep being the kiss that keeps you lying next to me before we dream.

I'll keep you close. Right in the crevices of my heart where you have always belonged. I'll take my skin off with you and share the nakedness of souls, the way we should. There isn't anything inside of me that you haven't already seen, and that's how we continue to be with one another. Because we promised the face of vulnerability and honesty. This is how we will be; I will love you here, and you will love me there.

I just want to love you, my dear.
You awakened so much inside of me,
and all I want to do is keep chasing
that feeling with you.

And when we kissed,
we birthed universes
that still continue
to swim around me
when you are not here
to make them move.

I love to live in bridges of certain songs.
It carries a piece of life that I want
to relive, over and over again.
It’s a moment of madness that births ecstasy.

I choose to love too quickly because it's the only way I know how to love. And even though it hurts more than it heals, I wouldn't stop my heart from doing what it's designed to do. Because giving is far more important than receiving.

And if you see that this love
is too much for you to carry,
let me hold it for you.
I can be strong enough
to love for the both of us.

Sometimes I am more closed off than open. Especially after there has been a difficult breaking of my heart. It can be hard to look at someone and want to let them in, because the cycle of breaking is there in the midst of so much hope. You see them, their eyes, the curve of their lips, looking at you with the unknown lingering in between. And you see the hope that is pouring out. So much damn hope that it drags down any kind of doubt that tries to drown out the light raining from the sun. And with a weak soul, I will give some more, even though it feels like it isn't much. I will give to you, my lovely. So you won't be without.

There are many types of love in this world,
but when it comes to yours, I sink into this
space of unearthing that has belonged
to us since breath first filled our lungs.

The sun and the moon know my heart so well. They know the way that I love you because it is the way they love each other. One belongs to the dark, and one belongs to the light. But in spite of their time apart, the sun dies every day so the moon may live. And the moon dies every night so that the sun may live. They live a life of sacrificing themselves so the other may breathe. This is how I love you, because you are worth dying for so you can live. A constant cycle that seems like the only way to be. We are as natural and extraordinary as the universe, and so we will live here in this beautiful madness living and dying for one another. Because for us, we have loved far greater than the walls of this universe could ever hold.

#iamsoinlovewithyou

If I were to walk on my own,
I would still be able to feel
the way your hands made
their mark on me.
Fearless we loved,
endlessly we shared,
boundless we meshed.
Tracing the moonlight
across our landscapes
and burning away
the loneliness of
untouched skies.

You are a beautiful thing all on your own, my love. I know you feel that people look away when they see the scars your heart has been carrying around most of your life. But I have not. I have seen the way the world has carved its name into your bones, and I see the way it hurts you on days when you can't stand to face the day. Sometimes it's all too much, and I only want to hold you longer and show you how much meaning you give with just a simple breath. There shouldn't be a moment when you think I would turn my back on you. It would be impossible to do so with someone who has seen your demons, looked them in the eye, and forced them to sleep so that you could breathe.

#iloveyou

It was all truth, all the things I told you. The way I love you isn't about material things or the flowers I have at my table. It's about the decision to stay through every single moment you feel like you aren't enough. It's about the nights I get to lie next to you because you are the arms I need to get through the night. It's about the unexpected adventures that take us to nowhere just when the world is starting to break us down in this somewhere. I want your heart. I want to keep this place in your soul. Because you are enough. You never give yourself the credit you damn well deserve. You are so much in one person; you are so much soul in a world of selfish skin. The hope I have is that you would see how worthy you are to be loved entirely, and with fierce passion and devotion. I just want you to love yourself as much as you say you love me, because in this kind of depth, there is no way to deny its existence. You just flourish in it, no matter the situation you're in. Souls were made to love as deeply and as much as they want. Even if our humans are the ones that get in the way.

Catch with your heart
what you can't with your hands.

Do not break
what you never
intended to love.

It is strong.
This love she has for the one
who holds her heart.
As the ocean grows in waves,
her heart wades through the
caverns of his soul
to find her way home.

I have learned
that being in love
with souls is how
you know what
it's like to be
genuine.

There were never stronger towers
than when his arms held her while
she was falling apart.

Love them for their beauty
Love them for their beast.
Or don't love them at all.

I will still be here with you.
We have been here before, where the silence
grows so loud that words mean nothing.
Yet, we still find ourselves surrounded
by the hearts that scream to stay close.
There is a constant sowing of seeds
we keep planting in this thing we
have yet to give a name.
Because it's so much more than what
love defines. But day by day there is growth
and beauty in everything our mouths
touch, and with the stroke of your
fingers across the sun.
I find you here with me,
in the chaos of eclipses
and the burning of stars.

#parastin

I'm a mess sometimes, I know.
My need for your attention is high,
and sometimes I can be too much.
But I am who I am, and I can endure
so much that you need not underestimate
me on. I love fiercely and without a second thought. I am a forgiver and believe in the power of being graceful. I will give you chance after chance because I would want the same thing. And above all, I won't give up on you.
I will fight for you and for us.
Because you are worth it.
You are so worth it.
And because I want you.

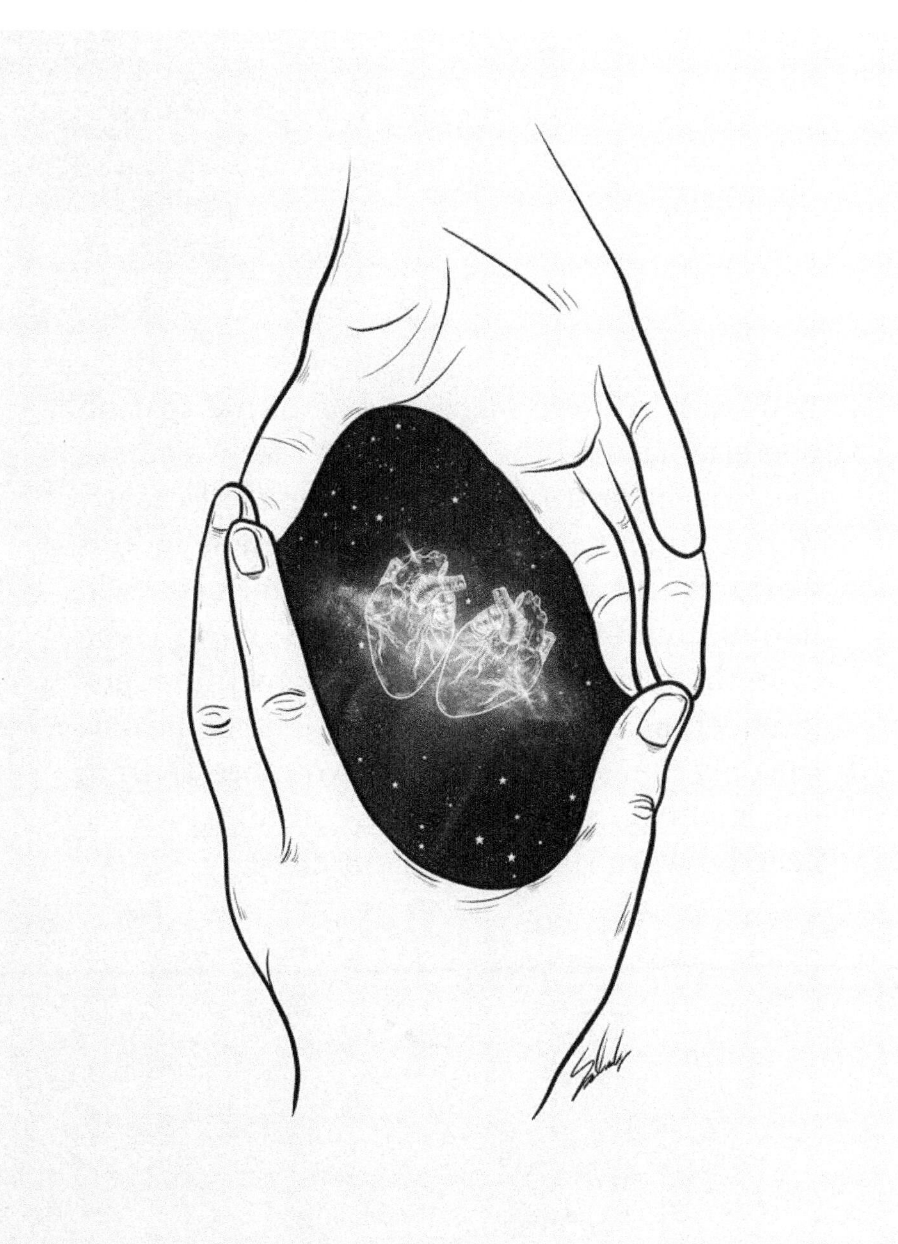

You exist in these places inside of me that no one else has had the bravery to reach. You see me, you listen to me, and understand exactly who I am. The most intricate design in this world is the connection between two twin flames, and the way we both have given everything we have to one another without any kind of hesitation. Because at the end of the day, the only thing needed to carry your breath from one night to another, is the constant love we keep between the bones in our chest.

#redamancy

I'm the kind of girl who stares at sunsets and would pull off on the side of the road just to capture the beauty. I would stay out all night just to watch the stars, until it was time for the sun to come up. I will crash into the universe every chance I get, because there's nothing more magical than taking in the pieces of the world that take your breath away. I'm the kind of girl that will savor a bottle of wine to myself, just to pass the time at a new place, in the quiet, to make a new memory.
Sometimes magic is about the things you can see, feel, and touch. And sometimes magic is everything you can't touch, see or feel. But know without a shadow of a doubt is there.
That is the beauty of this world, this universe.
And I am completely blown away by it all.

I would lay my life down for you.
I would give every piece of me
so that you could have more hope.
I would sacrifice it all to meet your needs.
You deserve to be shown that your life
has meaning, great meaning.
And you deserve to have someone
show you that with all the power in their will.

The first kiss was an awakening. From the way his lips molded with mine, to the way his hands pulled me in like I was meant to belong there. It was only a matter of days before the time we spent a part wouldn't be in vain anymore. There were only so many more nights spent sleeping alone without the warmth of his kiss on my shoulder, setting me on fire just enough to dream in sunsets. There were only so many more visions these eyes must travel alone through before they can know what it's like to explore with more than two hands. Certain forces must find their way through the dark of lonely before they can dance together in shameless light.

There was a kind of world she carved into her bones that made stars come alive. The type of power that ignited her life to the point where her blood ran in constellations and her tears created time zones.

Look at me again but linger this time. I want to just keep our eyes locked for a little while longer this time. Make your face flush with how open my heart is with you. I want to touch your face with grace and kiss your lips with complete assurance. Because after we give what are souls have been craving, there's no need to want for anything else.

She was not soft.
She had edges from the years that were not kind to her. She has scars on her heart the way a cutting board has its marks from the ones who came, only to leave.
She was not soft.
But she was strong and steady, because that's what life has called her to be. It was her perseverance that made her into the driving force that she is now.
Her roots were deep because she kept digging and digging until the wind only moved her branches and not her roots. Her name is virtuous and holds the definition of warrior. Which meant that her life consisted of wars that she would constantly be living and learning through in between each breath.

#eshetchayil

We were just standing there,
not doing anything but
holding each other in the shower.
And in this moment in time,
it was everything perfect.

She isn't half of anything.
She's the whole damn
Universe.

You can sit and watch the world go by,
and it can feel like the shortest yet longest
moments in your life when it's spent with
someone you truly love.

Peeling back your heart
for love will be how the
light of life gets in.

When you kiss me,
I want no other
taste to take my
breath away.
Fill my senses
with every bit
of your star
saturated skin.
Heaven is in you,
you make me feel
it while spinning
my world around
until I explode into
constellations.

#basorexia

She's the type of girl
that asks how you are
with every intention
of hearing how you
really are, what's going
on inside you, what's taunting you.
She puts your demons to rest
the way no one else has,
because no one has ever tried.
She is the part of the story
you can't wait to read more about
because you read truth in a world
full of fiction when you look
into her eyes.

You are the stars
in my sky and the
breath in my lungs.
My starry night,
branded in
forevership.

There is a safety in love,
because of the way
our souls reflect
that we are meant
to have each other.

#latibule

Being capable of loving
beyond what your heart
is able to hold, is the kind
of bravery we should be
spending our lives chasing.

That's what you didn't understand.
I would sacrifice everything I am
and all that I have for the sake
of loving you whole.

I travel through what seems like
a closed space to capture things
that ignite my heart.
There's this place I have found
where my breath leaves me
to be with the stars.
And the longer I stay there,
the more I long to live there.
Even though these places
are temporary, being in the
midst of it feels like a forever
home I was meant to stay in.

#acatalepsy

She was drawn to the things,
the spaces, the magic of
untouched skies, and the kind
of stars that held 11:11 wishes.

You will always be the soul I can't live without. No matter the road we walk down, it will forever be you with every twist and turn.

The beauty of this life
is that we are made up
of star matter.
A beautiful glow of dust
whisked together by skin,
and propped up by the
beat of our hearts.
How mesmerizing is that?

All love is dangerous.
Yet, that has never been enough
to scare me to stop myself
from loving you.

Sometimes I just want to
take a walk through the stars
and collect a few to save
and press in the pages
of my favorite books.

Twirling around in the kitchen
with a glass of wine in hand,
is my favorite kind of date night.
Because he makes me smile
so much, my cheeks hurt,
and I'm able to fall asleep
with nothing but content
in my heart.

#sozzled

Plot twist:
this life can be
whatever you
decide to make
it. Don't be afraid
to do, be, and chase
all the things your
heart desires.

Kiss me like dawn is waking you up each day.
Touch my face with your fingertips like my skin
is crying out for you.
Do you hear my heart beating
faster as you draw closer?
Do you feel my breath get heavier
as your hands start to move?
I can feel the stars start to envy
the love we make each night.
And it makes me smile
to know we have something *as beautiful as Us.*

I pray that my lips are the last you taste in this life, and that the love we create ruins you to every other soul in this world.
Because that is what you've done to me,
the moment my eyes saw you, my soul knew
it had finally found the meaning of living alive.

Love the strength that is you.

Let's start with the hard part.
Show me the sides of you that aren't
so pretty, the moments where you can't
bear to let me in, the times where the silence
is so thick in your throat it brings nothing but
tears.
Tell me what created the scars you wear,
so I can see the kinds of demons you face.
I want to start growing my love right there.
Because nothing is overlooked, ignored,
and walked away from more than the sight of
of the hard side; the dark side of our human.
Let me show you what it feels like to have
someone stay when they promise to.

You are worth having.
You are worth getting to know.
You are worth keeping.
You are worth the hard work
it takes for the long term.
You are worth it.

I want a day to lay in bed all day.
Where all we do is lay and stare at
each other, marveling at the world
we have created together already.
The way our souls continue to fly
along so effortlessly, weaving, meshing.
Creating sunsets and picking stars out
to hold in the box on the nightstand
for when the dark is too much.
I want to lay here with you
and just marvel in your presence.

She is too much heart
in such a small space.
Yet she keeps expanding.

His arms were the haven
needed at 3 am when the nightmares
are screaming. It's his touch that
parts the demons and unshackles
my feet from fear. He's the kind of
safe you can risk it all for, because
he's not there to just win you over
like a trophy. He's there to be your
best friend, the person you want
to run to because he's the first
thought above the rest.

He needs you just as much as you need him. Especially on the days when it's difficult for him to face another battle, another war inside his head. Lift him up with soft hands, pour into him as he pours into you.

I am softer at heart
because there are too many
hardened people.

I don't know anyone
else but you.
A heart like yours,
a soul like yours,
I simply drown in.
For as long as I have
these wings, I just
want to spend the rest
of time flying through
the universe with you.

Jump with me this time.
Give yourself enough courage
to face this unknown with me.
I know it won't be easy,
and I can't promise at times
it won't hurt.
But I just want you to know
we would make it through.
Because that's what you do
when you love someone.
You jump, I jump.
Remember?

#ifyoureabirdimabird

I am too much heart and soul,
full of second chances,
good intentions,
and deep love.

"you're not bored with me yet?"

I looked at him with disbelief that he would even think that. Our world is made of our own kind of routine, with a bit of spontaneity. But never boring. The nights we share with a bottle of wine, my legs over his lap, stained lips, and full hearts. You can't tire from love that's real. And the little things that make up the days and nights are the things that make up the whole picture. I cherish the seconds we fill, because even if the moments seem the same, it's still different because it's another day spent with the person you so deeply love more than anything.

Take a moment
and breach my soul.
Walk along the lining
of where sane meets
the intense.
I can show you things
you've never seen before.

Grab my hips and pull me into you, love.
I want to wrap my legs around you,
lips on my neck, hands gripping my thighs.
Spin me on my axis, eclipse my ecstasy.
Rise and fall with me, no walls
will ever be able to hold us up with
the way we make love.

I grew out of my fear when you showed me the other side of it. For so long I had not known how to breathe without my breath being laced with fear. Now my heart doesn't race so fast, I don't feel like crawling out of my skin when I must walk alone. Sometimes it only takes one soul, opposite your own, to show you everything you've been missing.

I look back at these years that brought us to where we are right now. The way we have fought to stay together no matter what, because we couldn't imagine a life without the other in it. No matter what was done, we stayed.
Loving through all the hard times that tried to tear us apart.

We stayed. We loved. We made it work.

We captured our moments
in small polaroid's and hung
them above our bed.
So we could dream of sweet
memories while we drift
off to sleep.

Ever so
close
we are
without
touch
without
sound.
Just
utter
soul.

An extraordinary thing happens when a woman is fully comfortable with herself. She lives her life the way she wants without giving two thoughts to what anyone else thinks. What an extraordinary power.

I was taught to always tell the truth.
Because it's always better than lies.
So here it goes;

I love you.
You're all that I have on my mind.
You're all that I want in this life.
I think you are the most precious
thing that the universe has
graced me with.
I am hopelessly mad
for the utter chaos
that we are.
And I want you
forever.

The best part about it
was how much you made
me feel whole.
Whole in the sense that
I didn't need anything
or anyone to fulfill
the parts of myself
that only God could fill.

I don't tell you I miss you enough.

The truth is, I miss you

All. The. Time.

#tumemanques

Love her when she comes home and tears her work clothes off to be in her favorite comfy clothes and fuzzy socks. When she throws her hair up, grabs a bottle of wine and crashes onto the couch. Love her when she's a mess of a thing, while she covers her neck in icy hot, with her mouth guard in and life is shut off. Love her for the way she is when no one else is watching, because that is when she is as real as it gets.

And when it gets harder to fight with you,
I will embrace you harder.
Stick by you when they say to run,
love you when they say to let you go.
And when it gets more difficult to look at you,
I will close my eyes and kiss you until the hurt
is healed with the way we seal our lips-
like a love letter written on tear-soaked paper.
And when I don't feel the love on my fingertips,
I will touch your face, and soak myself in the
entirety of you, while falling back into the
stupor of sinking into what belonged to me all
along.

When it comes to the red wine,
she makes you believe that miracles
can be found in the middle of a bottle
and in the stains that mark her lips.

I would
cross
moons
for you.

#selenophile

She found solace in the pages of old books
in the window that spilled her favorite kind
of morning light. The world is simple there.
Because it was her own world, scattered with
suns, and splashed in stars.

I want to get
lost on unpaved
roads with you
so we can find
the places where
stars shine
the brightest.

You were sunshine.
This is why I loved
you so much.
Because despite
the darkness,
you still let
the sun be
stronger.

Poetry is the written
truths of the things
our hearts have a hard
time putting into words.

It started raining inside of our apartment
because we willed our souls to be adventurous.
To become addicted to the things that matter,
instead of the things that fall away.
I love the magic we bring into the house when
we wanted the stars above our bed.
It was a box of cheap string lights we went out
in the middle of the night to get, because you
always told me you would give me the world.
These are the ways we make the
happiness eternal.

She gets paper stuck to her lips
in the midst of taking stardust
and sprinkling it out onto the
world with ink and laughter.

We didn't know anything
other than the way our
hearts started to dance
when we finally got to
be our real selves without
any kind of reservation.

Her favorite part of the fire
is the way it crackled beneath
the moonlight.
It perfected the pieces of
memories being created,
and to her, that was just
everything.

And if it wasn't real,

I wouldn't feel this way.

"I followed the moonlight."

She chased the beauty of the
untouched and marveled
at the light it brought on
sleepless nights.

#astrophilia

Inside the glasses of red wine
we find a certain kind of grace
that takes us to a place no one
else could understand.
We find our own flight
to freedom in full belly laughs
and the vulnerability
between each glass.

She learned how to have her own boundaries,
not to keep people out, but to make sure the
right ones were the only ones who could come
in. The years have made her wiser,
and have made her understand that
just because you see the potentially
good in someone, will not make them
treat you the way you wish to be treated.

Just to hear I'm needed
Just to know I am loved
Just to be held in your arms

there is nothing else
        in the world that I want more

Sometimes happiness is in a cup of tea
and the way the sun rises without question.
It's the kind of magic moments I try to
collect so the end of my life will have a
treasure chest full of all the things
I have ever loved.

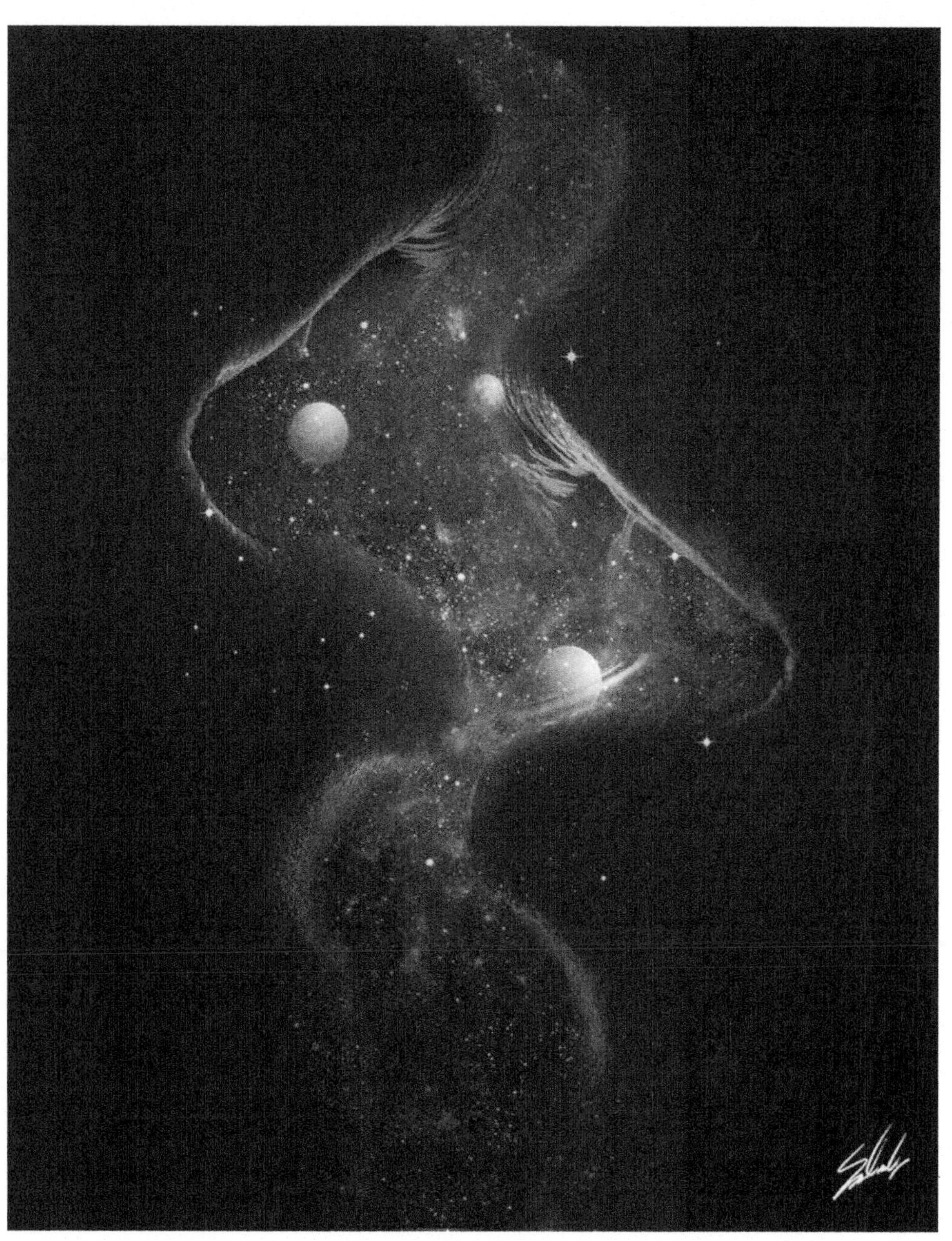

You make me want to open my mouth
when you cup my face with both hands.
Like your touch is my automatic surrender.

During the day, my thoughts are of you.
I can't help but float away in dreams of you.
I can't help but want to be with you.
Because close is not close enough,
and our skin is too shallow to hold
the spaces our souls are trying to reach.

#wonderwall

She didn't want a perfect life at all.
She wanted a life full of everything.
The choices that turn out to be mistakes
yet turn into new beginnings.
The love that gets lost, and the love that stays.
The terrible friendships that lead to the better
friendships.
She wanted the adventures that lead to
nowhere but end up somewhere.
The long conversations that make your heart
ache.
And the tears that make the night go by slowly.
She wanted the heavy weights of the storms,
and the calm of ocean.
She wanted the happiness and the sadness,
the sun and the moon,
and everything in between.

There are bad days that can be easily fixed with a glass of wine, the comfort of Greys Anatomy, and fuzzy socks.

He wasn't perfect,
but he was *my kind of perfect*.
The kind that doesn't see
a way out when things get hard.
The kind that speaks without
knives on his tongue.
The kind that takes me to places
that broadens my mind, instead
of caging it.
The kind that I can place my hope
in without worrying it'll be misplaced.
He was the way I look at the sky,
full of everything I love.

#myperson

Angels were made to fly through
the highest of highs while going through
the lowest of lows.
This is how they strengthen their wings.

She lives bottle to bottle.
Linking the legs,
studying the notes,
and memorizing
the way the flavors
take you into a
whole new place.

Fall with me here,
in this room,
in this space.
Fall with me in used
books and morning coffee.
Let's take ourselves
to other worlds, rummage
through the galaxies,
and rip open the sun
to see what's inside.
I want to make something
beautiful out of today with you.

She learned that life isn't about sharing your wings, but about showing others how to grow their own.

I only wish to swim in the depths with you.
So deeply that we float in the midst.
I just want to be terribly lost with you.

Gravity shifted when she decided to stand up for herself. She chose herself this time. After years of being torn down and told how she wasn't good enough, there was a moment that brutally awakened her. That was when she knew her life needed to change to be what she deserved. So she picked up her heart, tore down her fears, and stepped into the season of change her soul could blossom in.

And when you twirl my hair
with your finger, I swear
I lose my reason to breathe.

It's the music that gives you the kind of vulnerability that's sometimes hard to get from another human. It's a release of all the things you have trapped beneath your skin. All the chaos pent up in the pieces of a broken heart. It's giving confusion a name when there's a lack of understanding. It's scraping the wounds of old and making them feel again. Making the pain a beautiful rhythm coursing through the difficult tears falling off your face.
Music is the life given after death and music is the death of words, and the amplification of feeling.

#lisztomania

Your eyes held the sea and me.
All the waves that crashed,
crashed you into me.

The remedy to life is in the moments
we stop to appreciate all the blessings
we have.

I didn't plan on loving you this much.
But somehow you slipped between my
walls and fed love to my parched soul.
And I have been nothing but an
overflowing well since.

If champagne carried anything,
it's the magic of happiness
in bubbles and giggles.

You are my favorite soul
in this world. Because we
found a way where there
was no way, and became
a forever muse flying on
the back of the wind.

I don't have many words at the end of the day.
They are caught in the music tousled
up in my hair on the ride home.

I would give you my happiness on the days you didn't feel full of the sun. You deserve every bit of what goodness is.
And I could spend all the moments we have, giving you what you need when you can't find the strength to give it to yourself.

Even when it's darker,
I hold out my hands
and the moon still
gives me light.

We were more ourselves out in the country. Taking the long bumpy roads out to sanity, escaping the chaos that constantly surrounded us. We could escape there, we could be ok there. And it was everything that made us whole.

When you walk on the stars, you come to know God. You walk blindly by faith while He lays your path. The journey is untouched because it is meant to be marked by you. You see, dreamers like her memorize the stars and galaxies by name. So you can come back to earth to show how magic is already out there. We just have to find the courage within ourselves to dare to go out and find it.

It's always in the eyes;
that's where love dives its hands
and starts to change the beat
of your heart.

I am endless soul
and unwavering love.
Watch how quickly
I rise after being caged
for too long.
You'll find me
amongst the moon,
moving oceans
like I was always
meant to.

If all I was able to do in this life
was hold you with my gaze,
I would make sure the heavens
blushed with envy.
Because darling, I could stare
at you forever.

How hungry your lips are,
when they are starving for more
than just my kiss.
How moving your hands are,
when they make more than just
my legs shake.
How much I long to make
the ground quake beneath us.
Oh, how moving your spirit is
with mine when we crave
to make ourselves free.

I miss you during our fights,
because I only wish to be closer
to you when it feels like we're
being pulled apart.

I have traveled through ocean skies to find your sea green eyes. Just to hold you while you crumble, while you weep, and while you ache. Your pain does not go unnoticed, my love. I feel it when you need me most, and as I promised, I will always be here to help the pain go away. Even if I can't make happiness stay, I will hold your sadness to the light so you can feel the way the sun smiles for you.

You give me new ways
to burn brighter when you
tell me the ways the pieces
of your heart carry my name.

To be able to live this life,
knowing you're here with me,
living too.
I don't think anything
has made me happier.

Drinking stars is how I pull fire
into my soul. It's the light that
gives me hope when there's
nothing but darkness
consuming me.

It's a wonderful world,
when your eyes are lit up like stars.
It's a beautiful sight, the way your
whole body stands to talk about the things
you love. It's a glorious moment, to walk beside
you while holding your hand.
It's the little things that make me
gaze at you for just a few seconds
longer just to see the way you're smiling.

The moon and I
became very good friends.
For she was the only one true
in every end.
moonlit dreams

You are my morning prayer.
My soft love, with fierce hands.
My long-lasting sunset ever falling
upon my heart.
You are my place of peace,
the only calm that can settle my storm.

She was as courageous
as the stars.
Fearless in shining
just as she was.

The magic of it all
is that you hold my light
without ever trying
to dim my shine.

There is a map on my skin that I continue to follow. And as the years go by, my skin sheds, and my map changes. These are the changes I look forward to. This is the path I chose for myself. Constant change with the same core foundation leading my feet.

I won't let you leave, darling.
I'm strong enough to handle this. I'm strong enough to hold on when your grip is slipping. We've been here before. When it felt like there was no hope left, that there was nothing to hang onto. But there is always something to hang onto. Not just the love, but the promise I made when I poured out my soul to you.
Loving you is a promise, it's an act of living.
So I won't let you go, even when you pull away from me, my hand will still be touching you while you gather your thoughts. When you need some space, I'll still be there when you come back. Because we all have those times where we can't seem to be all there, even for ourselves. And sometimes it's ok to rely on the other person to love a little more, a little louder, and little harder. That is what it means when I tell you I won't leave. I'll be the anchor to keep us steady, so neither of us fall away.

You're my favorite flavor
of human soul.

#minutiae

Here and now,
in this haven of
your arms,
I find my shelter.
I find my peace.
And I am home.

You feel like fall to me.
The feel of a flannel on my skin while outside in the cold.
You are the cup of coffee in my hands, the gust of warmth that bleeds through my chest when I drink you in. You are the gust of wind in my hair, the shiver up my spine, the grip on my heart.
You are fall to me.
The season that sends me in a whirl of comfortable difference, absolutely full of the kinds of depths I stay in all year.

I love to capture our moments
in polaroid's, because they remain
untouched, unfiltered, and perfectly us.

I don't rely on your wellness to be good with my own, but it does affect me when you're not ok. It bothers me because I only wish for you to be happy. Even when I know that won't always be the case, I just wish all the good things for you, because you don't deserve any of the bad things.

I crave your scent;
every part of you I want
to feel in my hands.
mahogany teakwood

The walls have always needed a reason to come crumbling down. And when we find ourselves together, we hold the key to destruction. We find that our hands can't hold themselves still as they explore the parts of each other the world can't see. I make a move and you are already two steps ahead. Wrapped in your arms, we carry the torch to these walls, and burn them down the moment we touch.

With my legs around your waist, my hands holding your face, we drown in the making of love like a hurricane consuming the ocean.

I'm all about leaving marks on the world.
And it's nice to know your mark is on me,
because between you and me, I am your world.

I would rather have the mark of your mouth
stained on my neck, than the absence of it
with your presence.

Your heart is covered not only by your walls, but my own too. We go through this life together, and you don't go through anything alone because you have me.
There is twice the protection when you're a team, and twice the ammunition to fight back when there's an attack.

They don't tell you the good part about love. The part where even after you fight, there's the making up. The amazing sex that locks you back in after the fighting is said and done.
They don't tell you that sometimes the bad times are needed in order to become stronger.
They don't tell you how much happiness it brings into your life, knowing you have the love of someone who chooses to stay, day after day.
It really is a wonderful thing, having something so real.
Cherish it. Hold it close. And appreciate it.

I want to spend the day drenched in your lips. The flavor of your mouth pressed into my skin, and your hands finding themselves misbehaving. I want to be your good girl and obey your every demand. On my hands, on my knees, on this bed, or all over this floor. Make me yours all over again.

Nothing lasts forever, my love.
But I'll promise to love you
until forever ends.

It's easy to form a connection with someone when they touch the pit of your soul.
It's easy to allow their hands to come into your depths and lick the spaces that mirror the heart of their own. It is a fulfilling thing to watch the way soul mates mesh like the melting of gold into gold.

#raisond'être

What made you different from everyone else
is how you gave so much grace in the times
I did not deserve it.
And instead of holding it against me,
you let it go.

The need to take this love deeper
hung above our heads
until it all fell
from the stars
to drench
our
hearts.

Find someone who isn't afraid to feel for you.
Who doesn't hesitate to show you the way they
love you. Someone who you can fight with
without a fear of them leaving.
Find someone who chooses you, someone
who chooses you, and chooses you.
Someone who instills so much confidence
in you that when they say they aren't going
anywhere, you know it's true.
Find someone who doesn't make you question
where they stand. Someone who shows up,
every single day. Even when it's not easy.
Even when the day is busy and time is limited.
Because time is limited, and you deserve
someone who shows you their limited
time needs your presence in it.

I needed your stars,
not the space that
you brought
between us.

It was our own infinite dream
that brought our love to light,
and now we bask in the real
life version of everything
that's ours.

We have stitched
our hues to the
heavens so our
colors can learn
how to dance to
the rising of the
sun and shades of
the moon.

And just like that,
he kissed her like life
itself was in her breath.
Every wound was healed,
every lost dream came together,
and every piece of her broken heart
restored to be stronger than ever.

Somehow you turned
my soul inside out
when you pulled the
sun from the sky
and told me I was
a much better light.

I looked right into your soul
knowing every part of you.
I looked and saw you exactly
as you are. And I didn't want
to change a thing.
Because you're perfect to me,
exactly the way you are.

#kalon

You taught me that there's a happening when souls collide. Many hearts collide, but it's an earth-shaking move that bursts the universe when the right souls come together.

"I love you.
I truly love you"
she breathed.

"I am only yours"
he whispered.

11:11

Also by Kayil York

Roses & Thorns
Bleeding Caverns
You Deserve More

Featured in

Crown Anthology
And We All Breathe The Same Air

Find Kayil York

Facebook: Kayil York
Instagram: @rose_thorns1921
Twitter: @kayilcrow
Pinterest: Kayil York

Signed Copies:
kayilyork.bigcartel

Thank you so much
for your love
and support.

Love, Kayil
xoxo

Printed in Great Britain
by Amazon